SENSELESS MUSINGS

SHAKQILLE LEWIS

1st Edition January 2024

Book Design by Shakqille Lewis

Illustrations by
Jessica Lewis
Hollie Blake
& Jo Baddock

ISBN 978-0-646-89090-6 Paperback

Published by Shakqille Lewis
shakqillelewis@gmail.com

PREFACE

I am Shakqille Lewis and I claim absolute authorship over the words upon these pages and accept complete responsibility for recklessly unleashing their ludicrosity into the indie publishing abyss. I make no claim to distinguish myself as anything beyond an introspective tragic who finds satisfaction in sharing creative works of sincere expression.

Poetry is my excuse to write without boundaries and hide myself in plain sight. It is a treasure where I may completely expose the thoughts and feelings I'd rather not, and the ideas I often dress in humour for ordinary conversation. I now exchange such attire for the welcome vagueness of metaphors, allegories and unnecessary poetic flair.

These are my musings of the senseless variety and nothing more. I construct these sentences and sentiments without hope or expectation of anything except that someone, somewhere, at sometime may be influenced to think, feel or be as a result.

This collection is to be read, to be pondered over, to be felt, and to be forever intertwined within your heart and mind as a lexical bramble of thorns plaguing your soul ad infinitum. I request of you as a reader, to show me the kindness of reading slower, reading with considerate thought, and for the sake of all that is found in these pages—read these musings knowing they truly are senseless. Without sense not only in theme; but in structure, rhyme, metre and their loose adherence to the forever malleable definition of a poem.

My acknowledgements are so: A distinct thank you to Cinema which built my foundation for storytelling, Lyricism for nurturing my appreciation of inciting emotion and thought, and Biblical Public Speaking where I discovered my love of allegorical writing.

An honourable mention to my anxiety, depression and irresistible joy, for providing me with their inspiration, motivation, and unsolicited insight into my own humanity and the prejudices over my perceptions and judgments of worlds both external and within.

Without the friends with which I surround
myself the time required to truly gain
the comfortability to be who I am and
accept who I am not would be dangerously
increased; perhaps even indefinitely so.
It is for this I am immensely grateful and
of course, I guess, the addition of their
profound osmotic influence on my sense
of belonging (an illustriously elusive gift
many never attain) should also receive a
favourable mention. To you my friends,
belong constant sparking thoughts of you
and my raging affections which you may
find frightening, rightly so.

Only to my wife be unrestrained thanks,
the intense love of this madman and
irredeemable debt for her provisions of
ears to torture, mind to distill and whose
existence incites the following collection of
senseless musings of this fool.

> *"Poems are supposed to stay inside
> your head. Those who share them are
> pretentious."—Jessica Lewis*

THE MUSINGS

—POETRY—

—FICTION—

—POETRY—

Musing XVI (A Theme)

A theme unseen,
a theme unknown,
a theme does not exist.

A meaning unheard,
a meaning less bold,
a meaning does not exist.

      Within the poem,
       within the song,
    symbolism does not exist.

      Between the lines,
      beneath the words,
   the unwritten does not exist.

          the twitch of the lips
        the stress of the tone,
      the unsaid does not exist.

      Search for the hidden,
       see what you want,
          It . . .

The Person I Are

Am I Who I Am?
Or who I hope to be?
Perhaps I exist somewhere
in between?

The Light Of Darkness

True colours glow vivid in the dark.
If you see mine, tell me what they are?
Let the shadows seek out us.
It is the light which casts the shade.

No black can match the umbra inside,
I used to be afraid of the lack of light,
until it was that I realised;
I am the scariest thing in the dark.

To Notice

Walk into a room,
feel the wind change,
get a double-take,
and meet my gaze.

You seem kind of cool,
in a dorky kind of way,
just give me five minutes,
and you'll see we're the same.

Drawn in from your eyes,
your smile traps me in,
I've got no escape,
I forget where I've been.

I know the games you play,
see, I've played them too,
All I need is a laugh,
and then I've got you.

I'm zealous,
for the truth,
you hint at the notion
that I've gone and fallen for you.

Now you notice,
the rafter in your eye,
that's right, I'm cunning
and dragged you down with me tonight.

I knew I'd like your style,
by your glass of whiskey—neat;
smoother than the hand,
of aces up my sleeve.

Go and pick a card,
any card will do;
it won't change the magic,
I have in store for you.

I love the sweet emotion,
it gives me a kick.
The way milk and honey,
drips from your lips.

Shadows and flares dance on your skin,
running down your curves,
now they're making me—

Jealous,
over you,
electricity never hurt quite so good.

I watch you sway,
to the scent of the pines,
to the stars as they shine.

—All from walking into a room.

Glances

A word is uttered not to each other,
my knowing eyes glance to no other.
There wait yours poised for mine,
knowing glances on the mind.

Lingering smirks married
to no more expression,
breeds acknowledgement
with the utmost discretion.

Two minds craving
to be understood,
meld once again
like no others could.

Lending their eyes once more,
to the conversation sure,
not to have noticed their absence.

But their minds remain mended
as if the glance has not ended.
Just another interlink in their labyrinth.

Essence Of Life

To be without a dream
is to merely be
and nothing more than this.

To live without a dream
is in fact not to live at all,
but reside in unbearable existence.

Vampirical Zeal

I know there's an inferno within,
because the heavens brim
with billows of soot and embers.

It may be dormant and hidden,
but not yet for good riddance.
I'll stoke and poke its corpse.

Until your fervour soars,
and consumes once more,
I'll give breath to the kindling.

With hope that might
just ignite,
some explosive lack of apathy.

So strike not your match
with cool air that,
in despair would snuff your fire.

Oh do let me in
and I'll be him
that brings you back to life.

Love Me So I Don't Have To

I wish you'd worship my surface,
and I'll abhor my core.
Tell me you love me, tell me you want me,
all I hear is the roar

of the crashing waves over me.
Who is it they love,
this phantasmic identity?

A masquerade, a dance.
Am I who I have become?
Or is this but some tempting hope and I'm
the remaining sum?

Dance, dance, dance, keep up the show.
Upon those lying corpses,
lays this dancefloor of white snow.

Worship my surface all you like
and I'll abhor my core.
The hidden things are wickedly shameful,
who could know them all?

I am who I want you to see,
but will no one see me?
Will no hand stretch forth?

Beneath the earth's surface
is a hot driving passion
and unspeakable works of worth no more.

Can you love them? Can you hold them?
They require no worship,
unlike the surface.

But they demand restraint,
they beg for your kindness.
Do not abhor the core
for I have already fed it such in blindness.

A List Of Words For A Summer Night

Couple.
Empty.
Streets.
Stroll.

Humidity.
Cut.
Breeze.
Cold.

Night.
Moon.
Lightning.
Storm.

Dance.
Rain.
Bodies.
Warmth.

Lights.
Blurry.
City.
Sounds.

Puddles.
Splash.
Soaked.
Gown.

Run.
Rush.
Heart.
Head.

Laugh.
Hysteria.
Tears.
Shed.

Shelter.
Found.
Wind.
Swept.

Heavy.
Hair.
Socks.
Breath.

Loud.
Chest.
Minds.
Slow.

Tension.
Building.
Reservations.
Thrown.

Eyes.
Lips.
Hands.
Held.

Summer.
Evening.
Splendid.
Tales.

Complementing Views

"I do love sunsets," remarks the fool,
"paired with a summer breeze.
A sunset full of fire,
instilled with golds and pinks."

He looks longingly at his lady,
to the glisten of her rolling eyes.
"How do you like your sunsets?" he asks.
"With wine . . ." she replies.

Limerence

I want to be me,
I want to belong,
I want you to love me
as hard and as strong

as I'm thrown into you,
as I become absorbed,
hopelessly immersed
in a crimson chorus.

Is it but me,
am I the only one,
who wants every freckle,
who hungers the sum

of the lines of your curves,
the cold of your fears?
Let me drown
in the shapes of your tears.

I want the weight of your love
crushing my bones,
let me burn in desire,
let me be the cause

of all of your joy,
and some of your pain.
I ache for you to need me,
if it's all the same.

> Talk to me like your mirror,
> sing to me I'm your shower,
> put indelible ink to my chest
> for the power

> to truly know you,
> to make you my obsession,
> give you impetuous devotion
> and nothing less than.

You know I need the passion,
I do yearn for the flame.
Grant me the soul
hidden within your name.

Curiosity is all-consuming,
my restraint is at its end.
Pour me out until I'm
but dry bones of a limerent.

I want everything,
and I want it all,
let the river banks break,
let me see your raw

of those electric pools
full of star formations,
to gaze into forever
their brilliance I'll be sated.

I will strip you naked,
have you exposed,
Lay yourself bare
for me to know.

I'm drawn to your intellect,
I do love your kind deeds,
I want to be who you need,
But I need to die as me.

Have you? Can you?
Would you? Will you?
These are the musings
of a fool that dreams of you.

Let me bleed,
let me cry,
let me love to my grave.

Give me you,
truly you,
it's you that I crave.

Outstanding In His Field

A Scarecrow with talons
upon his left shoulder,
in the afternoon yellow
yearns of sweet whispers.

Crisper, steadily
the wind does grow stronger,
soon stars shall shine forth for him.

Dim the sun flickers
with daylight stretched thinner
as this guardian
stands out in his field.

Wield he does bravely—
solitude and strangely
none of what he expected.

Respected and feared
are twisted and weird
as virtues at the expense
of sweet company.

"Unto me," he pleads,
"heavenly obsidian steeds,
recline upon my bleached shoulders."

Older he grows
with a gentleman's crow's
talons gripped on their new haven.

Ravenous sweet whispers
melt his purposes,
to reveal belonging among the forbidden.

Malleable Light

Mirrors in your eyes,
mirrors in your eyes,
show me reflections,
reflections of signs.

Signs of the bend,
signs of the curve,
repeat you are certain,
certain you observe.

Observe without warp,
observe without fault,
light cannot deceive,
deceive you it cannot.

Mirrors in your eyes,
mirrors in your eyes,
caught in halls of mirrors,
mirrors of your mind.

Mind if they make me big,
mind if they make me small?
Funhouse of mirrors,
mirrors of what can you be sure?

Surely you'll insist,
surely you'll imply,
what you see must be so,
so I must be awry.

Mirrors in my eyes,
mirrors in my eyes,
filled with odd reflections,
reflections not your kind.

Cry they are weird,
cry they are wrong,
light is how you bend it,
I've bent mine into song.

The Intruder

A knife—a blade,
such a fascinating object.
A useful tool
and a suitable protection for some.

Yet, as it sits there
beside my pen-holding hand
I cannot help but succumb
to the chill of audacious nervousness
that bristles up my arm.

Why?

Not a being exists by my side
who would dare seize the blade
and drag its long curved edge
across my hair raised skin,
nor would I myself plunge
the dagger into my flesh.

Yet, there—the knife
sits beside my page-resting hand,
and I cannot help but fall victim
to the restless sea
which throws my stomach to and fro.

"Relief! Relief!" I cry,
through the echoed halls of my bones,
why—this torment overwhelms me.
Its absurdity,
its meaningless threats to my life
drive me to question my sanity.

I am in no danger,
I am under no threat,
and still lying under my tongue
is the anthem of intrusion.

What if?
What if this pen-holding hand . . . ?

Colours Of A Forest

—Rainbow
I sit at the foot of a tree—
just me.
I lean against its strength, wondering.
I wander about its forest and all its green.
Its scent is on me, the unfamiliar—
Peace.

In their swaying, release their lips
senseless things and childish fibs
giving such whispers unto him,
the one they call—
Zephyr.

Silence comes, and silence goes.
Critters hope to help me feel at home,
talking amidst the canopy,
sending good thoughts of their own—

—Orange.
Dust frolics in beams of gold,
settles on spotted creatures.
Lend their ears to birds of song,
whimsical be their nature.
They play by the water that shapes her
And it's here that she heeds my voice—
"Stay."

A standing ovation
my hairs express
when leaves squashed beneath
the boot I press
to a sound I so desperately need—
Crunch.

Rustle does carpet of beet-red leaves,
lemon-yellow, pumpkin and aubergine.
Let the fall rain down on me,
sunset is in the trees—
Can a forest cool a breeze?

—White
Logs hollow draped in moss and snow.
I follow silver trails of smoke,
to little friends in cosy homes,
indulging in their sweets—
Feast.

My mates they share their spoil and joy,
I lie down by their door.
Tree stumps used as tables,
my tattered fur our bed of warmth—
Slumber.

Run my hands over grain and ridge,
bark rough along my fingertips,
berry stains in their creases.
Bitter-sweet juices lap my tongue—

—Green
Fields wake and stretch their limbs,
Carmine red to violet hymns
the petals sing into the wind,
casting pollen lanterns up to the blue.
—Fresh.

I skip and trot with fawns and cubs,
coddled in their coats of love,
oh innocence with no fear of
all the things we've now forgotten—
Mist.

She holds me in her faithful arms,
the warm embrace of gentle psalms,
a life one could only ever dream of,
A band of colours never broken—
—Rainbow.

Sapiophile

Teardrop heat licks,
the waxen bed wick—
a luminary fastened to walnut grain.

While sweet emotion raids
your temple and evades
all its simple devices of resistance.

What is sacred I have venerated,
what is Holy I bless
and nothing is left unsanctified.

The temple's lips drip
with the glazen syrup
that shines with the vigour of honey.

That candle's malnourished light
is thrown into the night,
and the darkness plays its melodies.

And thus shadows and flares
dance upon your mind—fair,
down your arches to stir jealousy.

With aches brought forth
and no more thoughts
intrinsically laborious or burdensome,

linger I wish
you would longer and kiss
goodnight the fetters which bind you.

Let them fall by your side
and gloriously slide
the leaden ball in your chest beneath mine.

Cradle these dark tears
and caress my fears,
knowing they are all of losing you.

I'll do you the same
with ferocity not sane
for any man you did know.

I do pour some ivory
over porcelain curves and see
bonds of wax and skin flow forth.

Beneath your décolletage
beats a delicate heart,
I've never grown so envious of pearls.

Howl into the black,
toward the marble orb that
releases us under its glistening light.

And in the dawn somewhere,
approaches the star—unfair,
drawing our stage curtains closed.

A Story Of Old

Two souls dreadfully distinct,
with opposing dreams of being interlinked.

Amidst dark worlds, identities forged,
lives entangled forever more.
Waves of fire, flames of ocean,
a clashing symphony of devotion.
A story old, for belonging yearned.
Through blood their humanity is earned.

Two souls dreadfully distinct,
with bitter-sweet dreams of being
interlinked.

Shadow Of The Sun

Watch the sun over the horizon,
you woke up early
just to see its light come in.
It fills your world
with colour and brightness.
Can you see it yet?

Doing whatever just to stay alive,
it always feels like the longest night,
while the sun keeps
someone else's world warm and bright.

The sun always leaves you alone and cold.
His absence is growing while you grow old.
You say the night is dark and lonely,
I guess you never really noticed me.

And I try,
but I'll never keep you warm the same,
and I try,
but never will you feel the rays.

And I try, I do try,
if I could throw myself from the sky, I'd try
just so you could wish upon me as I fall.

In the night I shine for you,
but when the sun returns
his light is blinding you.

I guess it's just hard to be noticed,
it's hard to be loved,
when you're trying to shine,
in the shadow of the sun.

Not Yourself

So you're acting kinda weird.
Fighting back the need
to give way to your tears,
consumed by all your fears.

But they don't see,
they can't conceive.

Maybe if they knew your story.
Maybe if they knew
why you think how you do.

Maybe they would understand,
tell them because I know you can.
You're not yourself, you're someone else.

I hate the way you smile,
it's as fake as mine
but it's just not your style.
Haven't seen yours for a while.

But I'll hold on,
because I know it's not gone.

Maybe if they knew your story.
Maybe if they knew
why you think how you do.

Maybe they would understand,
tell them because I know you can.
You're not yourself, you're someone else.

Intersect

What could easily be mistaken for a shrine
is in fact a sanctuary of literature.
A throne stands solitary
among the endless shelves,
housing myriads upon myriads of books.

Bound by leather and cloth,
there are pages,
and bound by pages are words,
and bound by words is a story.

And when you open the binding of leather,
and of pages,
and of words,
you release that story.

Stories unlock the imagination of others,
tie us to the intangible,
an unveiling of worlds of the mind.
And especially appealing to my curiosity—
slowly finding out why they are.

It draws us closer to the thoughts of others,
But why is it so important?
Stories birth a magical realm
where we can be anyone,
and do anything.

Am I not content
with what life presently provides me?
Never!
How could I be?
My imagination is unbridled,
and my insatiable quest to explore ideas
and future possibilities
continues beyond comprehension.

It's a blessing to see a world of what ifs,
but a curse for them to fall short of reality.
And yet, somehow fables and tales pale
to the world that surrounds me.

Adventure

To live for what we know,
to explore a world unknown,
endeavouring to conquer
challenges unacquainted;

to hope for what we do not see
and daring to be enamoured by the miracle
of the marvellous wonder that is life;
this is Adventure.

The Glitter Strip

Cerulean waves invade
golden bands of sand,
ascending into dunes.

Further are the gentle trees
which march
up mountain ranges of great division.

And nestled between the blue,
gold and green
lives a strip adorned in glitter.

By day the ocean gleams
and so does the beach,
so too does the waxy leaves of the trees.

But by night,
it's the golden coast city that comes to life
as the towers shine against the stars.

The falling sun grabs hold
the mountain's silhouette
pulling it over as an emerald blanket.

And as its light follows,
the urban strip puts on its glitter show
from the theatre that is Cavill Avenue.

Ocean swell roars and applauds
with city sounds looming large,
welcoming the overcrowded.

Amidst the fairy floss sky,
skyscrapers rise high,
enveloped in clouds of salty mist

that grows fainter, with the blanketing
vapour giving over to warm lights
exposing a night of overwhelming flavours.

Engulfed are people
in booths of indulgence,
hedonism is the taste on their lips.

Inflamed by the tranquil
gratification of swill
burning in their chests.

Minds are enticed
by desirable sights,
dancers trapped in lo-fi sonics—dreamlike.

Dissipation and desire
swells in the embrace
of the deep pervasive bass

that rattles the bones,
intertwined
with a hauntingly audacious melody.

An explosion of the senses;
candy coloured glitter
sparkles in the hue of dirty neon.

While passion and satisfaction
are complemented by a lustrous rainbow
radiating from iridescent walls.

They must put glitter in the sunscreen,
it's in their blood,
as is the sand and surf.

Yes welcome
to the notorious land of plastic trees
and pool flamingos carved from marble.

Don't let the marvel of the sparkle deceive,
there's more to the play than the stage.
Glitter is not the city, glitter is not its soul.

Beneath the glamorous fabrications
is a beating heart—a voice;
Beneath the glitter is the gold.

Fireside

To what does fire owe
the mysticism it embodies?
The familiar smell,
the warmth of its embrace,
and the light it casts
is all nothing short of alluring.

But it's the way it moves—
an irresistible dance of flames
swaying to and fro in an unpredictable
ballad of organised chaos.

Controlled,
its hypnotic trance provides
a sense of safety
when coddled by its side.

And then—
and then there's a wondering
deep down inside
desperate to set it free;
to see when unleashed what passion,
what destruction
it is truly capable of.

Yet, there is a knowing,
keeping such urges at bay,
with the reminder the fallout
may just not be worth the reward
for curiosity.

Why do the beautiful always try hurting
me?

February Heat

Sausage sizzles in the morning light,
next to towered buttered bread of white.
I hear commotion from my pillow,
laying semi-conscious in my bed.

Blankets thrown to my floor.
Mist perches comfortably above my brow.
Given time I'm quite certain,
I'll have to backstroke through the air.

Wince I do with each foul strike
of hot air from the ceiling fan,
once a tool for keeping cool
has now betrayed its very purpose.

T'is the season for brilliant towels
tucked beneath the arm,
juggling umbrellas, surfboards and thongs,
all the while with swimmers on.

Radiators of tar have become the streets,
galvanised fences the children leap,
to pack into the narrow seats
of a family car fully-chockers.

Touching my side for a second no more,
the car belt buckle presses to my skin
with its hot unforgiving print
leaving me with its brand.

Leather seats stick to my thighs,
diesel engine warbles with the magpies,
pub tunes to which I know all the words,
Dad sings along to them all.

Fangin' across the blistering coals,
beaches coalescing of sparkling gold.
I think I've learned the path of hate
Anakin was dead set on.

A Sea of salt peppered in my hair,
its film holds to it crusty and dry,
with waves of spray rolling into the sky,
I'm lulled to comatose.

Grommets traverse the glassy pipelines,
ocean rises up under my arms,
my paddles deep in the water's warmth.

"This one's mine!" I carry on.
"Tell him he's dreaming," Dazza calls,
the firm sting of the sun grabs his arm.
Nothing sweeter than the thought of,
paddle-pops waiting for us on the shore.

Barbecue alight in fight with the campfire,
who can draw the larger crowd?
Existential bliss amidst friends fireside,
telling tales and telling tells, playing cards.

Is there a moment sweeter?
Sweating among friends after dusk?
Future fuel for nostalgia,
I think the heat is getting to my brain.

Bountiful Desert

On graves of sand,
two bandits land
in one quick-draw of the Royal Owl's hands.

And as he stands
in his cross-armed stance
his mind is in motion to execute his plan.

Before the other men can fire
and with no pause to admire
his work in ending the two bandits prior,

the hunter leaps at the leader
in his jet pack of silver
with a determination equaled
by no man meagre.

Carnal Cosmic Craving

I want that sunshine,
to drown in that golden rain,
I want that euphoric rush
that gives too much,
and adds to it no pain.

I want those pearly whites,
handing me the game.
So spread those lips
laced with this
pure serotonin glaze.

Give me that sunshine—
Electromagnetic ecstacy.
Send me the sunlight—
Its nuclear fusion dopamine.

Unfiltered sunshine—
Absorbed your eclipse,
Give me the sunlight—
Give me all of it.

My Star, I'm starving,
carve me off some of that Sol,
make it ultra-violent
I want to watch your finest,
light peeling on my floor .

Driven with hunger,
Let me wrap my teeth,
around your flares,
and if you dare,
I'll sink my fangs deep.

Give me your sunshine—
The lethal kind of dosage.
I need that sunshine—
This cosmic oxytocin.

I want the sunshine—
Pressed against the sunkissed glow,
Yes the sunlight—
We're the only ones who know.

You know I need to bask and to bathe,
You know I need your stardust to breathe.
You know I need bathing and the basking,
You know I will always be here asking.

The Entertainer

I am the greatest of entertainers,
the most hospitable of hosts,
to useless thoughts,
such useless thoughts.

They drink and they eat,
until drunk with gluttony,
the useless thoughts,
oh useless thoughts.

I ask them to leave,
of course never directly,
these useless thoughts,
my useless thoughts.

These rooms are filled,
and no seats are empty,
for useful thoughts,
dear useful thoughts.

Bruise with their laughter,
stab with their tongue,
in jest among mates,
they claim all in good fun.

Yet, I am left battered,
no bread in my jar.
Do dine, do recline,
please stay 'till the sun;

you useless thoughts,
oh useless thoughts.

A Lie Is Planted

He tells a lie.
He adds a lie.
He lives the lie.

He believes the lie.
He is the Lie.
All when he tells the lie.

It demands a dance,
of great expectations,
with twirls and dips
to a tempo most ferocious.

Happiness won't be found,
in the tune his feet now move to;
only a transformation,
can realities when fabricated give you.

Morph your face into that of a beast,
you cannot recognise;
whose company is of serpents,
destined to perish in escapable fire.

Proverbs Of Ashes

Am I the sea,
or just the monster who lurks beneath,
that you should set a guard over me?

Perhaps a couch will be my comfort,
I thought a bed would ease my misery,
yet I'm terrified by these dreams,
and ugly visions steal my sleep.

Suffocation is surely softer,
for my aching head to rest,
than this cursed body of mine,
oh this cursed body of mine.

So let me lie,
in this palace of ashes,
and draped in my finest attire,
sewn of sackcloth and rations,
of hardened loaves
so that I may loathe my life.

So, do tell me—
Am I the sea?
Or the monster that lurks beneath?
For all I see,
is a dark that must be,
of the ocean's deep.

Allowance

Am I allowed the lines
formed from a frown?
And proudly taste the salt
of tears upon my tongue?

My blood still gently oozes
the darkest cut of rubies,
and evermore so rudely
my dastard scars still itch.

Do grant me the kindness,
to gently take these wrappings,
and bind one's tattered sores,
with fabrics and cuts of cloth.

No.
In fact—wait.
I know who I am,
in time I'll bow to cowardice.

Sounds of pleading,
soon shall escape these lungs,
please I beg,
do stop your ears.

I plead you not
stop when I say when,
for such pain
belongs to this man.

My cries will be that of justice,
do not share in them.
Keep sympathies for one deserving,
not this wretched swine.

Curse me good,
and revile me well,
serve me the fruits
and the blooms of my harvest.

I dream of escape,
but I dare not deserve it,
I want freedom from pain,
yet there's suffering I'm warranted.

I aspire for nothing but peace,
and it does not belong to me,
for what I've done is the cause.

I know this pain is self inflicted,
but it still very much hurts.

Miserable Man

Here I am again,
miserable man that I am.
Bound to my back is the man I fight,

his burdens weigh me down,
I'd rather live without,
all his awful lies and vile cries.

His breath smells of decay,
his hands dipped in mud,
he's out for blood, looking to have me fall
to the man I once was.
The wars we wage erode my days.

The wars we wage erode my days,
the battles have me in a fog of war
in my mind is occupied
of things that were before.

I hate the way it feels good.
I hate the way it hurts.
I hate the starting over.
I hate that I deserve;

no sympathy,
no compassion,
no empathy,
just a ration of mercy and love,
and still not even those.

But . . .

I struggle for what's right,
my might refuses to fail.
Led by faith not sight,
an act of self betrayal

awaits me in the dark,
sharpening its claws.
As I turn to run
my anxiety soars.

Temptation crouches at the door,
it's craving dominance once more.
It's closing in on me.
It's stronger than I could ever hope to be.

It's getting closer,
breathing down my neck,
taking over.
Here we go again.

But . . .

I am given more,
and more I am given, still,
even with the man on my back
who I grieve will never leave.

But he will never be I, and I never him,
for with power from high,
for my life I will fight
the man that is bound within.

One Flesh

When you're on top of the world
the fall is far,
I thought clouds were made for my sleep.
It's the rushing air keeping me cool,
the earth is in a hurry,

to greet me without delay,
hurtling towards my place in the sky.
You snatched me from my descension,
you should have let me land.
Why teach me to fly?

Now you cry with all my broken pieces,
tar and sticky glues up to your elbows.
Deep wounds of red across your fingers,
my sharp edges you won't let go.
And now you're bled of your yellow.

You take me to your river,
drag my body through cold waters
hoping to wash me clean.
You should have let me drown.
Why couldn't you let the currents take me?

Now your hands are bleached,
your knees grazed and bruised
but my stains just won't come out.
I hoped you'd make a saint of me.
But that's unfair on you.

Even the devil tried
to trade the world's riches and power
for the integrity of one man.
If I could have yours I would,
but that's what makes it perfect.
Noone ever can.

So let me be free
to die in the bed I've made
to lay on the ashes of all that I've desired
to build and have admired.
Why didn't you leave me to decay?

Walk across my coals and scorch your feet,
carry me through our burning home,
rake me to your chest
and smell the singe of your clothes.
Yet, I'm the smoke
that suffocates and chokes.

Why wouldn't you let me go?
Why would you teach me to fly?
Why couldn't you let the currents take me?
Why didn't you leave me to decay?
Why won't you just let me die?

And now here I stand over you,
the silver of a sword weighing in my hands,
running the shadows of monsters through,
in this weary land
of terror
as your slayer,
indebted, I pledge.

I will fight,
until the rivers run bright,
with their stolen light.

I'll bear this shield
until their hordes bow and yield
and I'll make the gleam
of this armour seem
like the sun is the second coming of night.

I hold to nothing more righteous,
I keep to nothing more bound,
that the princess rescued the knight
in shining armour
with her kindness,
and with it,
integrity he found.

Farers of the Sea

Did you know?

I could walk your steps forever,
journey their spiral into every corner,
watch paint dry in every shade of you—
on the walls of our innermost rooms.

And did you know?

That I could stride with the hunger
of wanderlust to discover
what is the greatest of frontiers
ever unknown to humankind?

I do know;

Woman and then Man,
were made to be together,
not compete with one another,
but to complement and to be complete.

And I do know;

My Love and this Fool,
know our roles and play them well,
sail this ship against the swell,
hauling coruscating treasure
atop an ocean stirred by the sun.

You did know;

Always how to be brilliant,
in ways I love are different,
unique and simple radiance
unwavering in a world obsessed with black.

And you did know;

Of the lands we would explore,
worlds we hoped were sure,
sinking our feet in windswept shores,
an undying brimful of joy fills the sails.

Did you know?

This ship will always be,
our endeavours never cease,
and now these timbers are ever etched
with carvings of conquered seas.

Whippet Good

Bonds are born in the sands of a desert
where laughs are lost to the endless sky.
Rubber presses to the heat of asphalt,
carrying the lives of ten.

Gathered in the land of the big wet,
washing leviathans up the riverbeds.
Connection is under the stars,
with innocence lost in the virgin night.

Ruddy is the outback calling their names,
for the Joker and the Artist to take its hand.
Champions of consideration for the pack,
The Carer and Defender stand.

To observe is a love of the Investigator,
a true master of deduction.
Yet never could she tell the true shade
of green the Chameleon was always hiding.

Float does the Romantic with the Rock,
they doggy-paddle in volcanic warm pools.
Surely and certain will the Improver find,
a way so these moments we'll never lose.

And now it's the Fool in all his might,
driving his paws against the horizon.
It's with his pack of Whippets he belongs,
racing across the great red centre.

The Chameleon
The Joker
The Artist
The Rock
The Carer
The Improver
The Romantic
The Investigator
The Defender
and . . . the Fool.

The Safest Arms

I will always try to be
the man I never will.
I may ascribe it to arrogance,
or more accurately
your investments of faith in me.

I know,
it's easier to be alone,
than to be unknown,
to be unseen,
than to be forgotten.

Oh, I ask not,
to give me much,
but may these knees bleed,
the unforgettable aches
of my thankful heart.

For you subscribe,
that this life,
can still be more.

And for this,
I weep,
in warm arms,
of belief.

I'm yours.

A Poem For Jessie

To you is my affection,
In your direction
I send it on the breeze
which visits us in autumn
when it's just you, just me.

My gaze can be imposing,
I suppose it
can be much,
I cannot convince it to leave you,
But you could never trust

I would ever ask it
of a task it
couldn't possibly conceive
I'm forgetful, don't you know
when it comes to leaving you be.

I cry to the unseen above
that I do love
your will for what is fine.
Watch me struggle and strive for that giggle
to make my favourite blue shine

into my soul with all their force,
a chorus
knocking me to the earth,
where I will lay and listen forever,
entranced in every verse.

More than great lustre is their power,
devour,
they do my longings and thoughts
of unfounded anxieties
and other worthless sorts.

However did I find,
a mind,
with an intellect so brazen.
I guess I'm a sucker for a gal with wit,
to ignore, would call for treason.

I know a world persists,
to exist,
within your sunkist walls.
I'll pioneer in the name of exploration,
I will heed its call.

I found you,
all of you,
and made you my home.
In my deepest adventures,
I know with you I belong,

with that heart that beats repeatedly
and undefeatedly,
in the rhythm of ineffable kindness.
And a selfless nature of which makes me
nauseous of the jealous likeness.

Between your fingers are mine,
the divine
surge has never left this fellow,
but courses through each nerve and vein,
instilling absurdity in my marrow.

Tease my heart if you dare,
and tear
the restraints I self impose.
give me even, the implication of a reason,
to let these floodwaters loose.

I know you do adore,
this dork,
and all his awkward charm.
I hope you read this with his resting smirk,
Cause it's all for you my darling.

Chariot Of A Juggernaut

The fury of a storm surges at my back,
carrying me to frosted peaks.
Its relentless rage and determination
mightily rise from beneath.

Let me give in,
do allow me to rest,
I beg and plead with the storm.
Neither mercy
nor such fine sympathy,
does it unto me outpour.

Frigid fingers claw to the frozen gaps
desperate for some crooked crack to grasp.
Gingerly treat my extremities.
Ginger please grant in my tea.

Woe to the face that opposes me,
grant it strength against this tempest.
Heavenly light of brilliant strikes,
thunder pandemonium and due madness.

Helplessly swept into the windstorm,
taking even the anchored and the bound.
Give in to its sheer hallowing call,
for no refuge is safe nor sound.

Throw does the wind,
to heights unknown,
refusal is utter refuse.
Mountains and sky
sit at my feet,
and celestial jewels I choose.

To adorn the awe of heaven's crown
and bask in the glory of cosmic gowns.
But I do not seek this to attain,
some undeserved sense of fame.

It is the clouds bestowed on me,
a low that raises me high.
For when I'm weak, I'm powerful,
and on the storm I will rely.

I do not claim its fury,
not its power, nor its will.
I am but a vessel,
to this righteous cell.

Absurdity & Wit

I listen carefully,
I listen intently,
my ear is unreservedly inclined.

Though your sentence—incomplete,
and your words you repeat,
I've reached the finale in my mind.

To be so audacious
and with a speed outrageous,
I cannot resist to know.

Albeit how rude,
to boldly assume,
to be wrong is never on show.

So I wait a while,
and put to trial
the potential for such change,

But never arrive
does diversion of mind,
only my extrapolation parade.

Not To Fight But To Reason

Excuse my amusement,
I was simply mistaken.
I thought I was engaged with a man;

one qualified to defeat me
with considered thought,
convincing reason,
and a well trained tongue.

I now see who stands before me;
one who never learned to be strong,
never taught to exercise will,
but as even the weakest of children,
this brute is reduced to fists and rage.

Strike me down
and prove your worthlessness.
Boast in your ability to inflict pain,
a skill easily found, and readily hated.
Your greatness is as whitewashed graves.

Indeed, do find me a soul,
who can persuade and inspire,
do find me a heart,
that shudders with another.

To the world this one shines,
as an illuminator,
a gentleman who has learned
to effectively express.

Consider your next action wisely,
for it may decide truly
whether oneself is a man
or simply an oaf-sized child.

Endure, Persevere & Rejoice

To My Incomparable Defender,

Be glad if you receive this letter,
because I have endured to the end.

Cowards cannot break a spirit,
they can only swing their axe,
their tongues are lame and clumsy,
blinded by rage of misplaced fear.

Children with sticks and rocks,
hurl them at shadows and sounds,
they murder in the name of life,
they sin in the name of what's Holy.

Yet, it is hard to hate your enemy,
with insight inspiring understanding,
so then understanding brings forth love,
and love is the Conqueror Supreme.

But this integrity is built,
with unshakeable strength,
and Father has taught me well,
to stand firm with my face to the wind.

I beg of you,
do not be afraid
nor be terrified,
for an everlasting crown awaits me.
I will die as the man I hoped,
I will embrace death as me.

Death is but another enemy,
that will taste its own sting,
and drink its own venom.
My Brother is near,
and in his right hand,
he holds liberty from the grave.

This life I lay down,
was never mine to save,
and it was always fleeting.
So I exchange it for the promise,
of one more enduring.

Your foundation is immovable,
I know your heart is incapable of surrender.
It is not my love which sustains you,
but yours, but His.
This is our very purpose,
For this we exist.

I will endure under tribulation,
I shall persevere in prayer,
I will rejoice in the hope,

I will see you there.

With Inextinguishable Love,
Your Fool

Truth

We are all prisoners
to our own perception of reality.
Limited by the truth
we believe to understand,
convinced it is so.

The rose coloured iris of a man
tells him the world is without bloodshed.
His brother with eyes of blue
doubts the existence of oceans.

The Woman Of The Hour

Tangerine dyes the western sky,
all while the dusk comes calling.
Laugh and cry, do Clock and I.
Upon the veranda we tell our tales.

I wonder if after all this time
her ticking hands tock faster.
Wishing I'd hold them in mine,
I'd teach them how to saunter.

Her time-filled face of timeless age,
hold reflections of my fading.
Now her numbers crave to behave
as if distance were a word unfamiliar.

Watching the circles her hands draw
having their diameters cut in half,
knowing with every day that's born
her arms spend less time apart.

Her numbers know what to show,
but their deception is ever growing.
And now although I feel I'm owed,
some mistaken sense of restitution.

And still I'm aware it's somehow me,
I know I've lost my eye.
I know I've lost the accuracy
for keeping watch of stolen life.

Yes, soon, as nightfall looms,
honest she'll always keep me.
Racing by she can only fly,
knowing nothing of delay.

In all our wrinkles—mine and hers,
she keeps me moving forward.
With temporal warp my mind is cursed,
so to her dial I'll stay moored.

And as I sit with my clock I find,
just as a mist so is my life,
knowing the hands that stole my time,
look not like hers but mine.

FICTION

Tunnel Vision

Snapped into a state of interjecting awareness, Emilia's mind steals her from the moment, standing back from the canvas of her adventure to see the paint drying ever so quickly. Ringing silence grows in her ears until the bulging veins and the prominent bone structure of her crewmates is all she can recognise of their urgent screams.

While an injured woman and the crew are barreling through the hallways like a patient ushered into an emergency room, Emilia's legs become hers no longer, in her internal analysis she gradually slows in her pace, falling behind the rest of the crew in their panicked stride.

Eventually she is reduced to a standstill, stuck in her introspection before the entrance of the hallway. Watching the rest of her comrades hurried away in their concern, she is left standing solitary under the arched door frame, losing them to the arterial halls of the ship that lie before her.

Isolated by her emotional walls and professional responsibilities she is buried deep in the claustrophobic void of the once busy cargo hold. With the crew's motion taken with them the sensory hallway lights extinguish, transforming the tunnel to a cave of absolute darkness and dousing any remnant ambience of company. Leaving her with an overwhelming emptiness—Emilia is alone.

Gazing about the cooling vacant room she catches a view of her reflection in the glazed wall beside her. Her sandpaper throat begs for moisture and her heart fills with icy liquid nothingness as she resistively views her distorted mirror image. While her physical reflection is clear and untampered, its distortion is rendered only by her own judging eyes.

Her clothes, her smile, the life she portrays—fallacious pipedreams desired so strongly their fictitious existence inadvertently adulterates her perception of reality. Charles, the crew, the future she fought against but finds herself so desperately hoping for—are they mad concoctions of a deluded mind deceived by her own longings for escape and family? Or perhaps a potential reality worth fighting for?

Peering into her reflection she runs her hand over the leathery hide of her jacket, pinching the snow white fur of its collar, rubbing the cloud of hair with her thumb. Her hand rises to her face, gently cupping her rose kissed cheek, its warmth a welcome contrast to the uncomfortably frigid air of the cargo hold. Looking her image up and down her physical touches do little to convince her any of it could be real. As much as she kicks against it she cannot see anything other than a pretender.

Her feet take steps she does not command; she directs her eyes forward to the tunnel she now walks down. With each step an intrusive clunk heralds the illumination of another motion sensing floor embedded light. Emilia needs not the assistance of the guiding lamps to know what awaits in the harrowing darkness.

Just as the foreknowledge of the approaching sound provides no calm at its obtrusive arrival, knowing what awaits her in the cavernous hallway's deep shadows gives no ease to withstand its impending approach.

Terribly wishing to remain in a state of perfect harmony of her lives old and new, she stays ignorant to the foundations of sand fleetingly supporting them. Finally the time has come to take her last step, the step turning on the last light, the last light shining a revealing spotlight on a choice she wishes not to make.

Paralysing—the inevitable future seizes her foot, leaving it suspended mid-step. She wants nothing more than to avoid what is to come but she knows she cannot loiter in this moment eternally. Even so, her thoughts engage in a filibuster before the court of her mind, delaying that last step for as long as possible. All arguments heard, there is nothing else to be done, the state of delay must meet its end.

Her limbs reengage, her reservations release their hold, and her foot falls to the metal grid of the floor. As a rising sun the sensory lamp fills the tunnel before her, shining a light upon the choice that now seen holds a repugnancy beyond what Emilia had fathomed. Two tunnels, one to her right and one to her left. A dirty fork in the road, an abhorrent crossroads.

The hallway to her right leads her to the medical bay with Charles and the crew. The tunnel to her left takes her to her room where her communications device and the Playmaker await her. One could lead her on an adventure as a larrikin of the Velvet Sparrow freighter with a swashbuckling Charles and his band of rascals. Living a life in the wilds of the Outerworld, revelling from one daring escapade to their next awe-inspiring caper. It is the only choice offering her a chance at friends, family, and maybe love.

But what if she is deceiving herself? What if this life—her crew, was to reject her as a fraud? She could never return to the other. It is a choice she had already riddled with doubt. A plaguing shrapnel of a thought of it as a fanciful illusion she is unable to purge from her hopes.

The tunnel to her left offers her a life she knows, a life she is good at—deception, infiltration, seduction, and assassination. Its security is warm, but its contents—stale. Its guaranteed acceptance of her return to the fold is a much needed comfort, but its lack of exuberance is brutally exasperating. It is a life she can be sure of; but one she has no desire for. Leaving her wondering— is this a life she must accept? Should she cross into the wilderness of the Outerworld and the promises that lie beyond or remain enslaved to what is familiar?

A tremor pervades her hands and the onset of tears burns readily behind her eyes. Instinctively she works to overpower the watery evidence of weakness. In almost every instance prior her manifested pain

has had no fight worth notice; however the
cause it now battles for calls for justice.
Pain warrants tears and tears cry out
for acceptance. The only campaign that
has threatened to make her human dies
today and its death a hope consuming fire.
With the power of this affliction her body
overturns the deeply entrenched walls.
Against persistent resistance tears slide
into her gaze.

"Who am I?" her lips press against the
tears between them in a whisper, their salty
presence proving surprisingly foreign on
the tip of her tongue.

Her hands grow still as do her eyes and
so her heart forgets to beat. Striking itself
over with many pains it throws her spine
into an arch, her elbows pull into her sides.
With sweat dripping from her every pore,
bleeding her of her will and her strength
until they are no more, her frame collapsing
into a standing slump. Hands unable
to hold her tears, her body erupts in a
shudder. Alone she weeps. Alone she keeps.

Without the stimulation of motion the floor lights behind her slowly turn off, one by one they stalk her. Rushed by the lack of light, the woman inside pulls Emilia upright. Unable to quench the force of tears she continues her path with liquid agony cascading down either side of her red ridden nose. Graceful even in the throes of being torn in two she glides to her choice, if it can be called such. Her hips and feet take her to the left, but her chest refuses to lead.

As she approaches the divide of the hallways her self control suffers a lapse in judgement, allowing her eyes to glance one last time to the future on her right. With this moment of weakness her arm projects out in a reflex, jarring her body as her insubordinate hand stages a revolution in its goliath grip to the flatiron divide.

Nevertheless it concedes, leaving Emilia to wistfully watch the dividing wall wash those words of such a future from her hands. If only it would wash those tortuously wonderful words from her forehead and if only it could wash the darkest of its ink from her chest. The shadows hunt her down the curves of the left tunnel, but she is not bothered by the pitch-black. She no longer has need for the light, not even the darkness inside can frighten her now.

www.ingramcontent.com/pod-product-compliance
Lightning Source LLC
Chambersburg PA
CBHW070329120726
47909CB00008B/2664